Herakles

by Simon Spence

Artwork by Colm Lawton

Copyright: Early Myths

First Edition

First Published 2016

ISBN: 978-1540857491

For Eimear + Eva

Welcome...

We hope you enjoy our story of the Greek hero Herakles.

For more information about the series and to listen to the pronunciation of the names, visit: www.earlymyths.com (sometimes grown-ups find these challenging but kids love them!)

Also, check out our books on the Apple iBooks Store & the Amazon Kindle Store.

For news of our current books or new titles, visit our website, follow us on Twitter or like us on Facebook!

w: www.earlymyths.com
t: @EarlyMyths
f: www.facebook.com/EarlyMyth/

Herakles

The trouble began when the Queen of the Gods, Hera, found out that the King of the Gods had a new baby boy called Herakles. She tried to do great harm to the baby by sending two snakes to his bedroom, while Herakles and his brother were sleeping. The slippery snakes slid under the door and tried to bite the children on their toes!

But Herakles woke up, grabbed the snakes, lifted them into the air and giggled with delight at his new toys! The Nurse who looked after the children shrieked when she came into the room, terrified at the creatures! But the brave boy laughed- nothing scared young Herakles!

As Herakles grew up he needed to be careful of his strength. He had trouble controlling his anger and one day he hit his teacher on the head with a musical instrument! He even hurt some of his family with his strong arms and so his friend, goddess Athena, sent him to see the wise Oracle, who could guide a young hero.

The Oracle told Herakles that he needed to do twelve jobs, called the "Labours". Each Labour would test his strength and power. Hera watched as the Oracle spoke and she smiled; she hoped Herakles would not finish the Labours, and he would never become a powerful hero.

Herakles travelled across the mountains to his cousin, Eurystheus. Eurystheus wasn't quite as brave but he really liked telling people what to do! He told Herakles about his first Labour- to fight against the deadly Nemean Lion! At first Herakles tried to use his bow and arrow to shoot the Lion but its skin was so thick the arrows bounced off.

Instead he wrestled him with his hands and used all of his power and might to beat the ferocious animal. He pushed him down to the ground and held on tight until the Lion's last roar. He took the Lion's fur as his new cloak and headed back to Eurystheus' palace.

Next, Eurystheus sent Herakles to kill the Lernean Hydra, a creature with many heads each one with a dangerous bite. They hissed and spat through their sharp teeth and Herakles brought his cousin Iolas with him for help. But when they chopped off the first wriggling head, a new one grew back as quick as a flash.

Herakles moved quickly, chopping the next head with his sword and getting Iolas to use the flame of his torch to burn the neck, so no more slimy heads would appear! One by one the heroes battled together against the Hydra's heads until it could bite no more.

For the third Labour, Eurystheus sent Herakles into the hillside forests to collect a Deer called the Hind of Cerynia. The hunter goddess Artemis, who lived among the trees, owned the Hind. She was not pleased to see Herakles or let him take the Hind and so she leapt out when the hero tried to grab the animal's golden horns and ordered him to let go!

But Herakles begged her for her help and promised to bring the Hind back after he showed it to Eurystheus. Artemis agreed but told Herakles to be careful- if the Hind was harmed in any way, he would be in trouble!

Back at the palace, Herakles showed the Hind to Eurystheus and then set it free again in Artemis' forest. But now for the fourth Labour Eurystheus asked Herakles to bring him the Erymanthian Boar, a fast and snorting beast which had sharp tusks and a biting snout. Herakles chased the boar across the fields until he caught it in his strong arms and lifted it high in the air. He carried it back to the palace and held it up as a prize, terrifying poor Eurystheus who tried to hide!

The goddess Athena ordered Herakles to put the boar down. He agreed, and he began to learn how to use his power but take care not to do harm to others.

For the fifth Labour, he travelled to help King Augeas. The king had lots of cattle who made a smelly mess in their stables. It was so bad that he could not get his cattle to go inside! King Augeas thought Herakles was mad when he agreed to clean the stables by the end of one day,!

But the hero had a clever plan. He used his strength to change the direction of a nearby flowing river and pushed it through the doors of the stable, washing all of the straw and mud out the other side. Augeas' son watched as the stables were washed clean. What a clever hero! Herakles pushed the river back into its place and headed home.

Eurystheus sent Herakles to the high hills for his sixth Labour, where he had to find and kill the fast-flying Stymphalian Birds. The birds had sharp teeth and razor-feathers, and could swoop down from the sky to hurt a passer-by.

Athena gave Herakles a special pair of clappers called the krotala, which he used to clap together and scare the birds from their nests in the trees. As they rose up into the skies, Herakles carefully fired his arrows, shooting the birds down one by one. They squawked and tried to rush at him but he was too fast & cleared the treetops with his bow.

Herakles was now half way through his twelve Labours, each time using his power and clever thinking to finish the job. For his seventh Labour Eurystheus sent him to the island of Crete to challenge the great Cretan Bull.

This animal was strong, full of muscles, and Herakles had to hold it back as it tried to run at him with its sharp horns. It snorted, snarled, and stamped its hooves. Herakles put his hands on each horn and slowly pushed the Bull back, wrestling it to the ground. He tied it up and brought it back to Eurystheus, before finally setting it free to live on the hillside.

King Diomedes had some wild horses with sharp teeth who could eat anyone who even got close. Eurystheus now told Herakles to go to see King Diomedes and catch his horses.

Even the King himself could not control these animals and so Herakles had to be very careful. The horses were tall and fast and he needed to use ropes to catch them, tie them up and make sure he didn't get a nasty bite along the way. He caught the wild animals and gathered them together in front of his chariot. Holding tightly, he controlled them as they pulled his chariot across the land, back towards the palace at home.

Hera was still watching Herakles, hoping that he would not be able to finish his twelve Labours. When Eurystheus told him to battle with the army of female Amazons and come back with the Queen's special belt, Hera watched and hoped to see the heroes lose. Herakles brought some of the best warriors with him and they finally faced the Amazons and their Queen.

The women fought with all their might but Herakles and his men were too strong. As they began to win, Hera disappeared into the mist, unhappy to see Herakles succeed. As the last Amazon was beaten, he grabbed the belt and ran back to Eurystheus with his prize.

For his tenth Labour Eurystheus told Herakles to go to the end of the world and bring back the cattle of Geryon. Geryon was a very unusual monster- he had one body but three heads, with six arms and six legs! When Herakles met Geryon he was surprised and didn't know what to fight first- which of the heads and arms should he battle with?

Herakles used his sword and fought bravely with each of the three parts of Geryon. Once he beat one of the heads and sets of arms, he moved round to the next one until he beat Geryon in three sword fights! Brave Herakles!

When Herakles brought the cattle back to the King, Eurystheus told him to make a long journey to get special apples from the garden of Hera. First, Herakles had to go to the giant, Atlas, who held up the sky to ask him the way. Atlas was very excited to help and offered to get the apples for him if Herakles took over and held the sky. Herakles agreed but when Atlas came back he had changed his mind- it was very heavy, so why not let Herakles hold the sky up instead?

Our hero thought quickly and asked Atlas to show him how to hold it properly. But once the sky was back on Atlas' shoulders, Herakles ran off with the apples leaving the poor giant to hold the sky once again.

Herakles had reached the twelfth and final Labour. Eurystheus told him to go to the entrance of the Underworld where the ghosts of the dead lived and to bring back the dog called Cerberus. Cerberus was not a normal hound- he had three heads, snakes in his fur and he guarded the entrance from visitors.

With Athena's help, Herakles reached the Underworld and spoke gently to Cerberus. He asked Persephone, Queen of the Underworld, if he could borrow Cerberus and she agreed, as long as he brought him back unharmed. Herakles brought Cerberus to Eurystheus, finishing his final Labour, and returned the dog safely to the Queen as promised.

Now Herakles was free but his adventures did not stop there. He married princess Deineira and travelled across Greece.

One day they tried to cross a fast-flowing river and asked the centaur Nessos for help. Nessos was half-man, half-horse and he told Herakles he would carry Deineira across and come back for him. But when Nessos reached the other side, he attacked Deineira and Herakles had to use his bow and arrows to stop him.

As the centaur died he whispered into Deineira's ear and told her to take some drops of his magical blood and one day it would save Herakles' life.

Never, ever trust a centaur! Nessos had told a lie and the blood wasn't magical- it was poison! So one day when Deineira tried to help Herakles, she mixed the blood into his drink and it made him so ill that he died. But as Herakles' family gathered to say goodbye, Athena guided him up to the heavens on the mountains where Hera stood to meet him.

Her anger had gone by now and she held Herakles' hand to welcome him in. Herakles, the greatest of the heroes, had become a god and lived forever more with Hera, Athena and all the other Gods on
Mount Olympus.

THE END

Some interesting notes for grown-ups...

Notes About The Myth:

The story of Herakles is one of the largest tales in Greek mythology. It has many elements and is a wide collection of stories. For this book I have focussed on Herakles and his Labours, probably the most famous part of his tale.

Our image of Herakles and Cerberus

c.520 B.C., F204 Louvre, Paris

There are many examples of the Herakles story in visual art, on vase paintings and in sculpture. On the right is the example of the Nemean Lion in art.

We also closely followed early Greek vase painting for the Cerberus image, with Herakles kneeling down in front of the hound (left). It is quite a tender scene even if Cerberus does pose a threat!

490 B.C., Penn Museum

Our version of the Nemean Lion

In these scenes, we took the vase paintings as our template, trying to remain faithful to the original but to update them in terms of characterisation and colour (see examples for the Hydra and the Hind on right). We followed the position of our hero and the creature in both of these scenes and where possible, we like to try to reflect

525 B.C., Getty Museum

5th century B.C., Louvre, Paris

Herakles and the Oracle, with Athena behind

some of the earliest painters' work in our images. However some of the scenes are a little trickier. For example, the episode when Herakles goes to the Oracle to learn his fate does not get much attention from vase-painters. Here we had to create our own painting of the scene, using written versions of the story as our guide. We used the same technique for the final picture of the book, where we followed the literature for the tale of the funeral pyre.

Printed in Great Britain
by Amazon